Foreman
Has a Backhoe

For Ethan, Logan, and Lucas,
may you always be builders and dreamers—JG

GROSSET & DUNLAP
Published by the Penguin Group
Penguin Group (USA) LLC, 375 Hudson Street, New York, New York 10014, USA

USA | Canada | UK | Ireland | Australia | New Zealand | India | South Africa | China

penguin.com
A Penguin Random House Company

Library of Congress Cataloging-in-Publication Data is available.

ISBN 978-0-448-46398-8 (pbk) 10 9 8 7 6 5 4 3 2 1
ISBN 978-0-448-47838-8 (hc) 10 9 8 7 6 5 4 3 2 1

Foreman Farley Has a Backhoe

by Jenny Goebel

illustrated by Sebastiaan Van Doninck

Grosset & Dunlap
An Imprint of Penguin Group (USA) LLC

Farley is a construction foreman. He has an important job to do.
He must organize the crew and equipment on this construction site.

He starts with a crane and wrecking ball.
Watch out, building, you're coming down!

Foreman Farley has a crane.
VROOM, VROOM, BEEP, BEEP, GO!
And on his crane, there is a ball.
SWING, BANG, SWING, BANG, OH!

With a smash-bash here and a smash-bash there.
Here a smash, there a bash, everywhere a smash-bash.
Foreman Farley has a crane.
VROOM, VROOM, BEEP, BEEP, GO!

What a mess! Foreman Farley calls in a bulldozer to clear the site.

Foreman Farley has a dozer.
VROOM, VROOM, BEEP, BEEP, GO!
And on his dozer, there is a blade.
CRUSH, PUSH, CRUSH, PUSH, OH!

With a crash-ram here and a crash-ram there.
Here a crash, there a ram, everywhere a crash-ram.
Foreman Farley has a dozer.
VROOM, VROOM, BEEP, BEEP, GO!

All that rubble needs to go somewhere.
Foreman Farley uses a dump truck to haul it away.

Foreman Farley has a truck.
VROOM, VROOM, BEEP, BEEP, GO!
And on his truck, there is a bed.
HAUL, LIFT, HAUL, LIFT, OH!

With a bump-dump here and a bump-dump there.
Here a bump, there a dump, everywhere a bump-dump.
Foreman Farley has a truck.
VROOM, VROOM, BEEP, BEEP, GO!

That's better. But to make things *truly* flat and smooth, Foreman Farley revs up the grader.

Foreman Farley has a grader.
VROOM, VROOM, BEEP, BEEP, GO!
And on his grader, there is a scraper.
GRATE, GRIND, GRATE, GRIND, OH!

With a scuff-scrape here and a scuff-scrape there.
Here a scuff, there a scrape, everywhere a scuff-scrape.
Foreman Farley has a grader.
VROOM, VROOM, BEEP, BEEP, GO!

Now it's time to start scooping out the foundation. Backhoe loader—dig in!

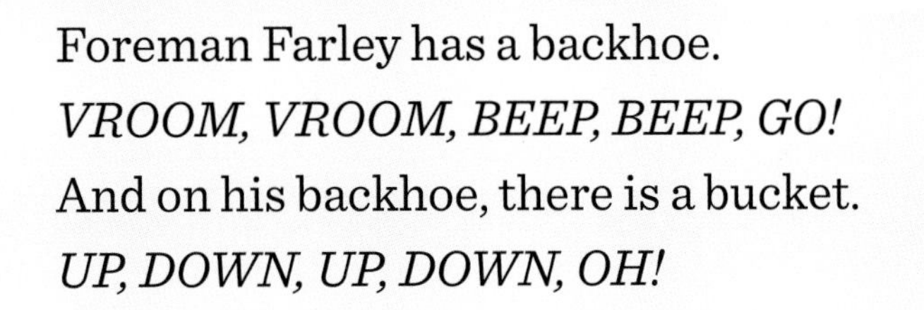

Foreman Farley has a backhoe.
VROOM, VROOM, BEEP, BEEP, GO!
And on his backhoe, there is a bucket.
UP, DOWN, UP, DOWN, OH!

With a dig-scoop here and a dig-scoop there.
Here a dig, there a scoop, everywhere a dig-scoop.
Foreman Farley has a backhoe.
VROOM, VROOM, BEEP, BEEP, GO!

What can pour a rock-solid base for the building?

A cement mixer, of course!

Foreman Farley has a mixer.
VROOM, VROOM, BEEP, BEEP, GO!
And on his mixer, there is a drum.
SPIN, TURN, SPIN, TURN, OH!

With a mix-pour here and a mix-pour there.
Here a mix, there a pour, everywhere a mix-pour.
Foreman Farley has a mixer.
VROOM, VROOM, BEEP, BEEP, GO!

Even Foreman Farley needs help.
His crew gathers around.

Foreman Farley has a crew.
VROOM, VROOM, BEEP, BEEP, GO!
And on his crew, there are hard workers.
HEAVE, HO, HEAVE, HO, OH!

With a grunt-huff here and a grunt-huff there.
Here a grunt, there a huff, everywhere a grunt-huff.
Foreman Farley has a crew.
VROOM, VROOM, BEEP, BEEP, GO!

Hooray! It's all finished.

And just in time—school is about to start.

Great work, crew! Great work, Foreman Farley!

BACK TO SCHOOL

With a crane and dozer, and a backhoe and grader.
And a truck and mixer, and a crew full of workers,
Foreman Farley built a schoolhouse.
VROOM, VROOM, BEEP, BEEP, GOOOOOO!